To Jack,
S.McB.

For Deirdre,
A.J.

First published 2007 by Walker Books Ltd
87 Vauxhall Walk, London SE11 5HJ

10 9 8 7 6 5 4 3 2 1

Text © 2007 Sam McBratney
Illustrations © 2007 Anita Jeram

Guess How Much I Love You™ is a registered trademark of Walker Books Ltd, London

The right of Sam McBratney and Anita Jeram to be identified as author and illustrator respectively of this work has been asserted by them in accordance with the Copyright, Designs and Patents Act 1988

This book has been typeset in Cochin

Printed and bound in China

All rights reserved.

British Library Cataloguing in Publication Data: a catalogue record for this book is available from the British Library

ISBN 978-1-4063-0453-4

www.walkerbooks.co.uk

GUESS HOW MUCH I LOVE YOU
in the
SUMMER

Written by
Sam McBratney

Illustrated by
Anita Jeram

WALKER BOOKS
AND SUBSIDIARIES
LONDON · BOSTON · SYDNEY · AUCKLAND

Little Nutbrown Hare
and Big Nutbrown Hare were down
by the river on a summer's day.

On a summer's day there are colours everywhere.

"Which blue do you like best?"
asked Little Nutbrown Hare.

Big Nutbrown Hare didn't know –
there were so many lovely blues.

"I think ... maybe the sky,"
he said.

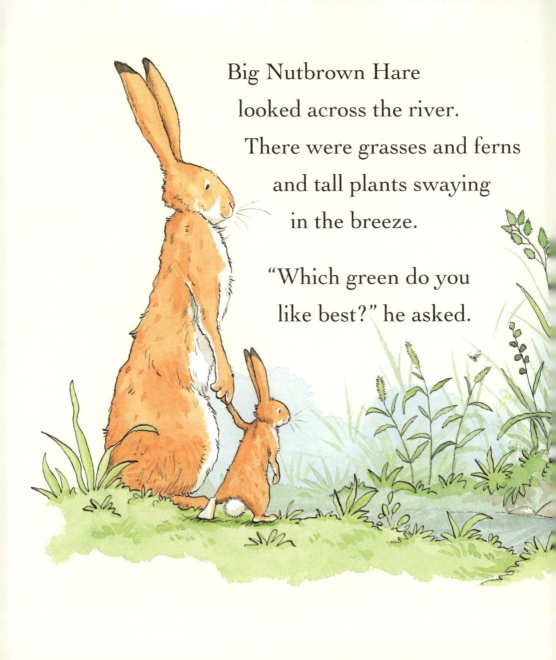

Big Nutbrown Hare
looked across the river.
There were grasses and ferns
and tall plants swaying
in the breeze.

"Which green do you
like best?" he asked.

Little Nutbrown Hare began to think,
but he didn't really know.
So many lovely things
were green.

"Maybe the big leaves," he said.

Now it was Little Nutbrown Hare's turn to pick a colour.

He spotted a ladybird, and some poppies.

"What's your favourite red?" he asked.

Big Nutbrown Hare thought about red things, but it was hard to choose just one.

"I think those berries," he said.

Big Nutbrown Hare nibbled a dandelion leaf.

"Which yellow do you like best?"

There were so many yellows! Little Nutbrown Hare even saw some yellows buzzing about. How could he possibly choose?

"Maybe these flowers," he said.

Then Little Nutbrown Hare began
to smile and smile.

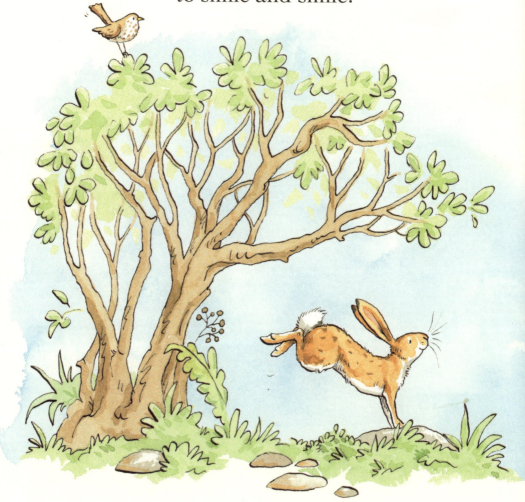

He looked at Big Nutbrown Hare and said,

"Which brown do you like best?"

And Big Nutbrown Hare smiled too.
There were many many lovely browns,
but one was the best of all...

"Nutbrown!"